The Big Fib

ROS ASQUITH

illustrations by Mairi Hedderwick

Barrington Stoke

First published in 2015 in Great Britain by
Barrington Stoke Ltd
18 Walker Street, Edinburgh, EH3 7LP

www.barringtonstoke.co.uk

The character of Robbie was created by Mairi Hedderwick for
Reading 2000 Storytime by Margaret Burnell, Sallie Harkness
and Helen McLullich (Oliver and Boyd/Longman Ltd, 1994).
Barrington Stoke gratefully acknowledges the origins of the
illustrations and the character of Robbie.

Text © 2015 Ros Asquith
Illustrations © 1993–1994 Mairi Hedderwick

A CIP catalogue record for this book is available
from the British Library upon request

ISBN: 978-1-78112-470-3

Printed in China by Leo

This book has dyslexia friendly features

To Lucille and Babette – R.A.

For Robbie again, of course – M.H.

Contents

Chapter 1
Click Clack

Robbie MacGregor lived in a tiny, windy, sunny village by the sea. On days when the wind was still, an interesting clicking sound came from Robbie's little house.

"Ah," the postie said as she delivered the mail, "that will be Granny Knit."

You may be wondering what on earth the postwoman meant, so I'll tell you straight away. Granny Knit was Robbie's mum's mum. Her real name was Angusina, so why was she called Granny Knit?

She was called Granny Knit because she knitted from dawn till dusk.

Sometimes Granny Knit knitted at night too, and the click clack of her needles kept Robbie awake.

Our story begins on one of those nights.

It so happened that a new girl, Anna Simpson, had started at Robbie's school. Robbie had been day-dreaming all day of ways to impress her. And now, just when he needed to sleep –

CLICK CLACK CLACKETY CLICK!

Robbie crept downstairs to see what Granny Knit was knitting. He peeked round the door and saw her stuff the knitting into her big knitting basket.

"What is it?" Robbie asked. "It looks like a woolly sunset."

"None of your beeswax," Granny Knit said.

Robbie knew this was Granny Knit's way of saying it was none of his business, but he went on asking until she said it was a new blanket for Annie-Kit, Robbie's cat.

Robbie was pleased, because he had been hoping that it wasn't another pair of bad trousers with kittens on them.

"Please don't knit so loud, Granny Knit. It's giving me knitmares," he joked.

But later that night Robbie woke up from a real nightmare where his kind teacher, Mrs Pine, turned into a scary monster that looked like an angry tree.

In his dream the tree monster shouted something that sounded like "GO! THE BELL!" or "NO YOU SMELL!"

Robbie's eyes snapped open and he woke up with a shiver.

What a relief – he was in his own cosy bed.

At breakfast, Robbie told his mum about the knitmare.

"I expect your dream turned Mrs Pine into a tree monster because of her name," his mum said.

"What do you mean?" Robbie asked.

"A pine is a kind of tree," his mum said, as she piled Robbie's plate with poached eggs, sliced mango and ham. Robbie's mum should have been a chef but instead she worked in the craft shop.

Robbie looked at the poached eggs and prodded the mango with his fork.

"Can I have toast and jam?" he asked. "Or a bowl of Flaky Corns?"

His mum sighed. Her lovely meals were wasted on her family. "I wonder why your knitmare monster was shouting 'GO! THE BELL!' or 'NO YOU SMELL!'" she said.

But Robbie had forgotten about his dream. His heart had sunk into his trainers.

'Oh no,' he thought. 'It's SHOW AND TELL today and I haven't got anything to bring to school. The nice new girl Anna might laugh at me.'

Out loud, what Robbie said was, "I've got a sore tummy. I don't think I can go to school today."

"Robbie, you just asked for toast and jam and Flaky Corns!" his mum said. "I don't think you have a sore tummy at all. You know it's wrong to tell fibs."

Robbie's heart was still in his trainers as he got his coat and school bag.

Just before he went out the door, he poured a little pepper onto his hand and gave it a big sniff. Then he trailed off to school slower than a slow snail.

Chapter 2
Like a Volcano

Just before Show and Tell, Robbie really did feel ill.

"Please, Mrs Pine," he said. "My tummy feels as if it's on a merry-go-round and my head feels as if it's on a big dipper." And then he gave the most enormous sneeze.

A-TISH-OOOOO.

"Atishoo, you need a tissue!" Robbie's friend Calum said.

"It sounds as if you're in a funfair, but without the fun," said Megan.

"More like a walrus playing the bagpipes," Archie joked.

Everybody laughed. To Robbie it seemed that the loudest laugh of all came from Anna Simpson.

But he couldn't stop. He sneezed again, even louder.

Megan pretended to put up an umbrella and the whole class roared.

"Now, that's enough." Mrs Pine shushed the class. "I think you'd better go home, Robbie. I'll call your mum."

By the time Robbie's mum arrived
at school, Robbie was sneezing every
two seconds. He sounded more like a
volcano than a boy.

"I'm sorry I didn't believe you," Robbie's mum said, as she tucked him into bed.

Robbie wished he hadn't sniffed the pepper. His nose was running like a waterfall and his eyes itched and dripped, and it was a lovely sunny afternoon and he was stuck in bed.

Chapter 3

The Great British Knit Off

The next day Robbie felt much better, but his mum said he still looked a bit peely-wally and he should have another day off school.

"I have to work in the craft shop today, so I can't stay home to look after you," she said. "Maybe your dad could take a day off from fishing?"

"Oh dear, no. I've got a busy day today," Dad said from behind his paper.

"Well, who can we get to look after Robbie?" Mum said.

"Granny Knit, of course," said Robbie.

Robbie liked it when Granny Knit looked after him. She let him play with her old wool and she made him yummy meals like fish fingers and beans and cake with custard (the custard was for the cake, not the beans).

"Robbie! That cold has given you a headful of air," Mum said. "Granny Knit's not here. She went off yesterday to take part in the Great British Knit Off. Remember? Last week she won the Highlands and Islands final."

"Oh dear, I hope she won't knit me any more bad trousers," Robbie said. "But I'm feeling so much better. Annie-Kit can look after me."

Robbie's dad chuckled. "Not the best plan, no," he said. "I'll give Uncle Poached Egg a ring. I'm sure he'd be delighted to spend the day with you. Just as long as you take his tall stories with a pinch of salt."

Dad ruffled Robbie's hair.

Robbie shivered. He thought he might never take a pinch of salt or pepper ever again.

"What do you mean?" he asked. "Why are Uncle Poached Egg's stories taller than anyone else's? Do you mean they are long?"

"No, your dad means they are not always true." Robbie's mum laughed, and she told him to zip up his coat.

Chapter 4

A Pinch of Salt

There were three excellent reasons why Robbie was happy to go to Uncle Poached Egg's house.

The first reason was that Uncle Poached Egg's house was full of strange and wonderful things that he had picked up on his adventures.

The second reason was that Uncle Poached Egg loved woodwork, so Robbie often got to hammer some nails.

And the third reason was Uncle Poached Egg's happy little dog, Porridge.

"I wish we could have a dog like Porridge," Robbie said.

"I don't think Annie-Kit would like that much," his mum said, as they reached Uncle Poached Egg's house.

Uncle Poached Egg was peering out the window, watching for them.

"Come in, Robbie," he said. "Guess what I'm making today?"

"It looks like, um, a little wooden curl," Robbie said. "What is it?"

"You be patient and you will see," Uncle Poached Egg said with a chuckle. "Now, did I ever tell you about the time I sailed to the Tropics and saved two beautiful young ladies from an octopus? And one of those young ladies was your own dear Granny Knit!"

"Granny Knit's not a young lady." Robbie giggled. "She's as old as a dinosaur."

"Aah, but she was young once – and as beautiful as the dawn," Uncle Poached Egg said. "Your granny and her friend were stranded on a desert island with not a bite to eat or a drop to drink," he went on. "If I hadn't sailed by that day, I fear they would be with us no more."

"Oh no," Robbie said. "That means I wouldn't have been born."

"Very true, my lad, very true."

Uncle Poached Egg leaned close to Robbie as he described the wild storm and the amazing rescue.

"The waves were as tall as a house and in the tallest wave was the biggest octopus ever seen, and it stretched out its 8 great arms ..."

Here Uncle Poached Egg waved his own arms, so it seemed to Robbie that he had grown tentacles like an octopus.

"I battled the octopus all by myself," Uncle Poached Egg said. "And all I had to help me was my old wooden box. It's empty now, but in those days it held a fishing net, like your dad's, but smaller and with magic powers."

"I netted the wild octopus," Uncle
Poached Egg went on. "And then I dived
into the icy water and rescued the young
ladies. Then I let the octopus go and
warned it never to return."

"But how?" Robbie said. "You can't
talk to an octopus!"

"Of course I can," Uncle Poached Egg huffed. "Don't they teach you anything at school these days? I can talk fluent octopus, shark and mermaid. My squid isn't quite so good, but ..."

"Go on, talk octopus then," Robbie said.

"Don't you want to hear about the pirates?" Uncle Poached Egg said, changing the subject as fast as he could.

"On our voyage home, we were attacked by a hundred pirates with gold teeth and red beards and wooden legs."

Uncle Poached Egg described his brave fight against the bold pirates.

When he had finished, Robbie said there was one thing he wanted to know more than anything else.

"What would that be?" Uncle Poached Egg asked.

"Why are you called Uncle Poached Egg?"

"That's a long story," Uncle Poached Egg replied.

"You mean a tall one?" Robbie said.

"Cheeky!" Uncle Poached Egg smiled. "I think it's time for you to play with Porridge."

So Robbie went outside and threw some sticks and Porridge ran after them.

'I think I will teach Porridge to play football,' Robbie thought. 'Dogs are more fun than cats.'

When Robbie came back inside, Uncle Poached Egg was still carving his little curls of wood.

"Oh do tell me what they are," Robbie begged.

"Very well," Uncle Poached Egg said. "They are ... curtain hooks."

Robbie's face fell. He had been sure
Uncle Poached Egg was making something
for him. But then he had an idea.

"Since you won't tell me why you're called Uncle Poached Egg, will you please please please lend me your little wooden box?" he begged.

"Why would you want that?" Uncle Poached Egg asked.

"For the next time we have Show and Tell," Robbie said. "I can tell my class all about your adventures."

Uncle Poached Egg smiled. "Why not?" he said. "But keep it safe in your bag, mind. Don't lose it!"

Chapter 5

Terrible Old Fibber

That evening Granny Knit arrived home.
She had won –

2nd prize in the knitted trousers Knit Off.

3rd prize in the tea cosy Knit Off.

4th prize in the knitted village Knit Off.

But Granny Knit wasn't happy.

"It was a disgrace," she said. "Violet MacPhee had knitted half her village before we started! I saw her pull a whole row of woolly shops out of her knitting bag! That woman is such a cheat."

"Never mind," Robbie's dad said. "It's not how fast you knit, it's how well you knit."

"Yes, you are the best knitter in the universe," Robbie said. "No one can knit trousers like you can."

As Robbie said this, he crossed his fingers behind his back, but he was pleased to see a smile spread over Granny Knit's face.

"Just think – if Uncle Poached Egg hadn't saved you from those pirates, you might never have knitted anything at all," Robbie said.

Granny Knit turned pink.

"Oh, don't you believe a word Uncle Poached Egg says," she snorted. "He's a terrible old fibber."

"He said you were as beautiful as the dawn," Robbie said.

Granny Knit turned even pinker.

"So if Uncle Poached Egg is always telling fibs, why doesn't he get into trouble?" Robbie asked.

Robbie's mum mumbled something about grown-ups and tall stories.

'Humph,' Robbie thought. 'If Uncle Poached Egg can tell fibs, then so can I.'

Chapter 6

Footsteps

Robbie decided to follow in Uncle Poached Egg's footsteps.

He knew he wasn't quite big enough yet to sail the seven seas and save beautiful maidens from pirates, but he decided it would be fun to play down by the burn after school and practise being a hero.

"I'll be a bit late home tonight,"
Robbie told his mum. She was looking
up a new recipe for scrambled eggs
with sardines and seaweed. "Archie has
asked me to tea."

"OK, but don't be home too late,"
Mum said.

After school, Robbie went to the
little bridge over the burn, where he
had played Pooh sticks since he was
tiny. He had never been there all by
himself before and it felt like a very big
adventure.

He imagined he was Uncle Poached
Egg, only the girl he was going to rescue
was Anna Simpson. Robbie flung down
his coat and bag and set to work. First,
he built an island out of big stones.

Then he made a boat out of sticks with a leaf for a sail.

His island swarmed with pirates – they were beetles in real life – and dragonflies and little fish made excellent sea monsters.

Robbie was so involved in his game that he didn't notice the time passing. He also didn't notice how slippery his island was becoming.

The stones were damming up the burn and the water rushed round and over them just like a raging sea. So when Robbie jumped onto his island to rescue Anna, he slipped and – SPLASH! Into the water he fell.

Two lucky things happened.

The first lucky thing was that the burn was shallow.

The second lucky thing was that
Robbie's neighbour, Mr MacReady, was
passing by just at that moment.

Mr MacReady hauled Robbie out of
the burn and carried him home.

Chapter 7

Fingers Crossed

At home, Robbie's mum was busy baking.

At half past four, she popped out to Mick's Stores to buy some cherries. She kept an eye on the road to see if Robbie was on his way home.

And who do you think was in Mick's Stores?

Archie!

"Where's Robbie?" Robbie's mum asked. "Isn't he having tea with you?"

You can imagine how worried she felt when she saw Archie's blank face.

Robbie's mum ran home to phone all Robbie's friends. She was just about to ring the police when Mr MacReady delivered a wet, shivering bundle of Robbie to the front door.

"How dare you tell such a big fib?" Robbie's mum said. She was furious.

"Get upstairs now and out of those wet clothes!" she went on, her face red with anger. She ran Robbie a hot bath with bubbles and scolded him the whole time.

Then she made Mr MacReady a cup
of tea.

In the bath, Robbie remembered his coat and bag. He had left them by the burn! And in his bag was Uncle Poached Egg's precious wooden box!

Robbie jumped out of the bath, pulled on his clothes and hurtled downstairs.

"Mum! I've left my bag by the burn. It's got Uncle Poached Egg's special box in and my spare trainers and my ruler and and ..."

But just at that moment the doorbell rang.

Guess who it was?

Almost all of Robbie's friends from school.

And they had his bag! And all his other things too!

"Everything was scattered all over the place, but we found it all," Archie said.

"Archie told us you were missing. We were so worried about you," Megan said.

And guess who was holding Robbie's coat? It was Anna Simpson.

"Well, you're just in time to have some of my cakes," Robbie's mum said.

The cakes were made from honey and banana, with coconut icing and a cherry on top. They were a bit sticky, but everyone was very polite and said how yummy they were.

That evening, Robbie's mum and dad had a serious talk with Robbie about telling fibs.

"I am very sorry for being so naughty," Robbie said, "because it made you worried and it wasn't safe. But still, you don't mind Uncle Poached Egg telling fibs."

'And,' he thought, 'we all tell fibs about Mum's fancy cooking sometimes.'

Then he added, "And we fibbed to Granny Knit that I liked those bad trousers with the kittens on that she knitted for me."

Just then Granny Knit came downstairs.

"Knitted trousers!" she said. "Did you want me to knit you another pair?"

"Oh, that would be lovely," Robbie said, with a blush. Some fibs, he realised, were told out of kindness.

"I think you've got the message, Robbie," his dad said. "And you won't be fibbing to us again, will you?"

"No, never again," said Robbie.

But he crossed his fingers and whispered, "Except about Mum's fancy cooking and Granny Knit's very bad trousers ..."

Chapter 8
Two Kind Fibs

There were two more kind fibs in Robbie's life that week.

One of those kind fibs was from Uncle Poached Egg.

You may remember that he had told Robbie the little wooden curls he was carving were curtain hooks.

But Robbie had kept on pestering him and at last he told Robbie that they were beautiful little coat pegs. He had made one for everyone in Robbie's class. Anna Simpson loved hers. And Robbie was very proud to have an uncle like Uncle Poached Egg.

And the woolly sunset that Granny
Knit was knitting? It wasn't a blanket
for Annie-Kit and, no, it wasn't a pair of
scratchy bad trousers either. It was a
jumper with a pattern of poached eggs
on it.

"Oh Angusina," Uncle Poached
Egg said. "That is the most splendid,
delightful and magnificent present I ever
did have." He gazed at Granny Knit as if
she was as beautiful as the dawn.

"And it is extra wonderful because it is made with your own fair hands."

"You silly man. You always make such a fuss," said Granny Knit. "It's made with wool and knitting needles!"

As Robbie drifted off to sleep that night, he thought how some fibs were for kindness, some were "tall stories" and some were bad fibs, like fibbing about going to the burn on his own.

Robbie wondered if Anna had been fibbing today when she said she'd like it if Robbie went to her house for tea. He decided that she wasn't fibbing, and that she wasn't telling a tall story either.

That night, the clickety clack of Granny Knit's knitting needles didn't give Robbie knitmares. Instead he lay in his own cosy bed and dreamed sweet dreams. He dreamed about pirates and a wild octopus, about storms at sea, desert islands and little wooden pegs made by Uncle Poached Egg.